Wildflower

Wildflower

A COLLECTION OF POEMS AND SHORT STORIES

DEBASREE GHOSH

PARTRIDGE
A Penguin Company

Partridge books may be ordered through booksellers or by contacting:

Partridge India
Penguin Books India Pvt.Ltd
11, Community Centre, Panchsheel Park, New Delhi 110017
India
www.partridgepublishing.com
Phone: 000.800.10062.62

Contents

Preface..vii

Poem 1.   The Rainbow 1
Poem 2.   Rejoice with Nature 2
Poem 3.   The Ponderous Evening 3
Poem 4.   A Tale of 2 Voices................................ 5
Poem 5.   Friendship.. 6
Poem 6.   Of Memories and Sea shells 7
Poem 7.   The Summer Night.. 8
Poem 8.   The Songs Unsung.. 10
Poem 9.   Voices from the Past 12
Poem 10. The Night Lamp................................. 13
Poem 11. Like a Vagabond 14
Poem 12. The Beautiful Truth 16
Poem 13. The Sea and the Sun 17
Poem 14. "An Exercise in Exaggeration." 18
Poem 15. The Spell of Morpheus................................... 19
Poem 16. Nature's Bounty 20
Poem 17. The Passer by 21
Poem 18. The Wandering Mind 22
Poem 19. A Kiss in the Air.. 23
Poem 20. Poetry in Nature 24

Poem 21. Winter Sunshine 25

Poem 22. Life is like that 26

Poem 23. You'll Never Be Mine 28

Poem 24. The Bench 30

Poem 25. The Irrational Love 31

Poem 26. In Memory of Mrs Chatterjee 32

Poem 27. The Startling Life... 34

Poem 28. For the Einstein at Einstein Centre 35

Poem 29. Love So Deep... 36

Poem 30. The Sun the Moon and the Sea..................... 37

Poem 31. A Riot of Disquet... 38

Poem 32. Another Evening.. 39

Poem 33. Reflection 41

Poem 34. The Journey Without an End 42

The Stream... 44

Just A Happy Love Story 49

Preface

This is my first published collection of poems and two short stories

"The last time I looked,

The flower was blooming,

It's thorns still young and green.

Life, like a desultory ghost was looming,

It's real form yet unseen."

Like the Wild Flower that grows in the wild, in the valley and in the meadow and atop a hill or floats on the river, poetry as well as the stories grew from within me naturally—they are not implants from without. The urge to write was natural, arising out of my experiences in life and how they got entwined with my emotions—my trepidations like the first time when I as a child hesitantly neared the water front and dipped my foot into the cold icy water, how these struck a chord within me and urged me to express my feelings. Slowly like the way a flower matures, the onslaught of varied experience moulded my thoughts and inspired my poetry. It continued to articulate my joy of unfurling the curtains of perception and sharing the joy of living and sometimes the pain that came with it.

Life has so much to offer and often so much to take away from us all. Our convictions, our doubts, our joy and our sorrow—all of them blend together in our quest for that ever eluding meaning such feelings hold for us—and what could be more beautiful and more lyrical than to express our innermost thoughts through poetry. Like they say poetry is magical!

This book is dedicated to all my loved ones who have inspired me to pen my thoughts

POEM 1

The Rainbow

The Rainbow is a memory,
Of all the days gone by,
It treasures legends of the past,
Whose souls enchant the Sky?
O Land of Colors and Mystery,
What secret do you hide?
Behind that blue-veiled curtain,
Which blessed being can abide?
The last time I looked, the flower was blooming,
Its thorns still young and green;
Life, like a desultory ghost was looming,
Its real form yet unseen

POEM 2

Rejoice with Nature

Our friendship tore, like a Muslin cloth,
On the jagged edge of a sea-shore rock.
I picked up each shred, in silent dread,
In quiet anger, in dismayed shock.
The waves were unperturbed, their routine undisturbed,
The sea-mist stole in at the appointed hour,
I sat very still, contemplating, until,
Nature's indifference held me in its power.
I roam the sands, till the grains rebuff my feet.
I greet each day in a philosophical way.
I think too much, 'but such is life
Meant to be,' I now see that
I've trained my eyes to seek answers in the skies,
To create reasons for the way things are,
I refuse to let unpleasant thoughts bar
The happy dances in my mind,
The faces of those who've been kind,
Those little gestures, to which I'm never blind,
The fragrant memories which have stayed behind.
And the not unpleasant shower,
From a monsoon sky.

POEM 3

The Ponderous Evening

There are just so many ways in which one can actually
spend an evening like this
. . . the best way, for me, is to spend it carefully, in idle
contemplation
. . . sometimes life is so mesmerizingly beautiful in its
connected wholeness,
In its infinite potential,
In its glorious epiphany,
In its stinging disillusion,
In its absolute absurdness,
in its incredible dynamism,
its beautiful stillness.
In the unsurpassed, surprised wonder of each new
friendship,
in the amazing incredulity of each newly-forged bond,
Each unthinkable kinship.
In the unforgotten poignancy,
In quietly treasured joys,
in its strange silences,
Its imagined romances
And deep introspections.
In the way in which life whisks us,
Across space and time,
Across people and places,
Across latitudes and oceans and unseen seas.

Debasree Ghosh

Over unknown meadows,
Far away hills, empyrean heights
And deep, sunken gorges.
I cannot quite understand,
And am trying in vain to figure it out.
Everything both makes sense and doesn't.
It seems to resist and invite interpretation
. . . so alluring and evasive it is . . .

A Tale of 2 Voices

A voice insistently lingers,
In a crevice of my mind:
And its silken fingers run,
Softly down my spine.
That hint of a quiver,
And that silent shiver,
Refuse to let me pine.
There flits a lone mistral,
A lightly tripping breeze . . .
A pastiche of past perfumes,
Which puts my mind at ease,
And yet
Does its best to tease
My soul,
By dividing it,
And yet
Making it whole.
There lilts an arcane melody,
Amidst the whirring of my heart:
Which matches the rhythmic beats,
With its tuneful art . . .
There lies a sleepless whisper,
In the depths of my ear,
Which keeps you locked in me
When you're far from near.
I can still hear that voice
Since you're far yet near.,

POEM 5

Friendship

I could only watch in silent, earnest despair
As our leash of friendship snapped in three.
Was it too passive of me?
Maybe we're much more free
And liberated this way . . .
I want to see the day
When we can smile at each other,
Rather sheepishly.
Not that I'm really sad or blue . . .
Sometimes
Life teaches you
To laugh when it hurts
And I think that
I may have mastered the art
In (rather irregular) spurts . . .
Though I do believe,
That friendship which is true
(Or Love, for that matter,)
Is cemented with a glue
So resinous
That it is hard to undo . . .
Much as you try . . .
"Love is not love which alters when it alteration finds . . ."
Is a line which to my mind very firmly binds.

POEM 6

Of Memories and Sea shells

'Thus says the man . . .'
Believe me, I loved her,
Beneath the feathered sky of a blurred-moon night,
The moon flitting in and out of sight,
Protecting our privacy, and yet
On guard,
To ensure all we did was right.
The sand grains were listening,
To our bare feet shuffling
Along . . .
Like two crabs . . . only
Our grip on love wasn't as tight
As theirs.
The stars looked dull and wistful,
and envious, even . . .
As she picked up a fistful
Of shells and sea-foam . . .
Now the stars were swaying,
Or 'was it' our heads?
While she was saying,
What I've never said . . .
That was the last day I remember with her.
It'll be sixty years ago this year.

The Summer Night

It is that time of the year,
When Spring slowly edges near-
-But not quite,
Though this spring might
Linger for a spell longer,
Than is usually right,
Being the remnants
Of the coldest,
Boldest Winter,
I've felt in a while.
In Summer, it takes me hours
To wade through the sea of time
To cheat the sun, to retreat
From the relentless heat . . .
Monsoon's tempest-toss'd nights thrill me
As I trace the tunes
Of nocturnal drops,
Which drench my dreams,
And tear into my sleep . . .
This Winter evening I walked several miles,
In the snug company of friends . . .
The chill of dusk
Settled around me,
Unsettling me . . .

Teasing my shawl,
Posing haughty challenges
To my inadequate sweater . . .
Imminent Night,
with its Falling degrees,
Was fast engulfing us
As we navigated our way through the darkness.
The mosquitos annoyed us,
With their incomprehensible melodies
Of harsh dissonance . . .
And amorous bites.
My ears rejected
Their bold proximity,
Their undesirable intimacy,
While they drained our blood . . .
Un-charming vampires of winter nights,
I'll settle for the Transylvanian Count any day.
The long dark evenings spill into the night,
Giving the sun's rays rather a rude push . . .
And the night steps in, its veil engulfing in on the city

POEM 8

The Songs Unsung

The evening pulls me into myself,
In silent contemplation,
In exhaustive introspection,
In quiet, private, expectation,
I will wait for you.
Though the days are blurred and hurried,
Though the hours are capped with work,
Though my songs are left unwritten,
As they die upon my tongue,
Though my thoughts are still amorphous,
They crystallise at times,
When I convince myself,
That the wait is worth the while . . .
I have a life to carve,
I have a dream to shape,
It may take me a while,
To realise what it was,
I will spend my idle hours,
(Though there are very few,)
I will re-construct my desires,

And wait the while for you . . .
I have a while to work,
I have forever to learn,
We all have livings to earn,
But I shall not yearn
For you,
I shall instead,
Wait in well-rehearsed optimism . . .
So when we walk past the lake of dreams,
Limpid with our love,
When we taste the bite of reality,
As we brush past its rude shove,
When we dance amidst the rainbow clouds of expectant
hopes,
When we avert our eyes from blazing, orange flames,
We'll be together, and our wait will be over at last.
If only for a while.

POEM 9

Voices from the Past

My heart aches, my soul breaks, the world shakes . . .
We just don't seem to have what it takes
To make this work out . . . I shout
At you, I even say a thing or two
I immediately wish I could take back . . .
I rack my brains to find a way to make it up to you,
The stakes are simultaneously too high and low,
I can, but can't quite let you go.
Will somebody show me the way to do things right? . . .
We fight and love with equal ferocity,
We epitomise reciprocity
And yet, we as a couple atrophy,
I might have worked this differently,
Had I another chance:
I would've re-worked things through a single, conciliatory
glance.
But it's a whit too late, much as I hate to admit it.
I'm not entirely sad, nor am I entirely glad . . .
I mean, you were a cad . . .
Or weren't you?

The Night Lamp

In the light of the tilted orange lampshade,
With the half broken bulb,
The words of the book
Stared dimly at me.
My eyes were swimming
In the blurred,
Artificial twilight.
My brain kept rejecting
The words, which tried
Forcing their entry:
My sleepy mind
The faithful sentry.
A night lamp is just not the way
To prepare for these tests every single day.

POEM 11

Like a Vagabond

Hand in hand
Over land
And sea
We
Travelled, the
Untrammelled
Bits of the world.
Round and round
Unbound
And free were we
As we
Strolled.
Him and me.
We had nowhere to go
But that didn't slow
Us down.
Not one frown

Of worried anger
Corrugated our brows
now
Was the time to roam?
With no desperation
To find a home.
To explore
And create
New homes, in new plots
Each in different slots,
Each called us with
A different flavoured voice.
Ephemeral
Seemed better than eternal.
Until we had to make that one choice.

POEM 12

The Beautiful Truth

Left and right the city breeze blows, scattering the scent of
the urban rose.
Even in the cold glare of the broken neon
Her face looked beautiful
Bereft
Of the glow offered by sunsets and half moons
Her beauty remained inviolate
And unchanged . . .
Being of a different breed . . .
A beauty which doesn't change
With time or settings,
Or the frail flicker of Age's flame.

POEM 13

The Sea and the Sun

And then he said . . .
"Let's follow the map of stars and go,
To that lone place only you and I know."
And so we ran . . .
To watch the soul-thrilling meeting of Sea and Sun,
Merging their bodies till they were one.
And soon we sat,
Beneath the un-intrusive Moon
On the soft, yielding sand—
While all the while did he croon
Magical Melodies as he clasped my hand.
And soon we lay
Our eyes searching the sky for a poem.
While the snow-capped waves bathed our feet,
Gently washing away our heat . . . .
I knew this wouldn't, it couldn't last . . .
But little did I know that
The spell would break so fast . . .

POEM 14

"An Exercise in Exaggeration."

My love is like a shooting star,
Sent down by the pale moon:
Gleaming like a heap of fine gold,
Upon a silver spoon!
I shall never stop loving "thee"
Let the moon in Seas' drown:
My heart's bonded to yours for-ever,
If the world goes up-side down.
If silver souls meet together,
To form a Golden Heart,
Ours will merge with one another,
Till from this world we part.

In Eternity, my fondest love,
Search not for my soul:
For I'll be within YOU, my love,
We'll exist as one whole.

POEM 15

The Spell of Morpheus

I wait for the sunset, search for the horizon,
Looking for unanswered questions.
Why can't I find them when I need to?
Around me the roses stir,
Aroused by an amorous breeze.
Around me the lone fly buzzes,
For once it doesn't irk me.
I'm too ready with answers.
But I can't find those questions,
Which had piled up, in
Dis-organised stacks.
Perhaps,
I'd left them alone too long.
Or maybe they were impatient,
And unwilling to wait a while,
Like most people I see around me.
Or maybe I'm just lazy.
Yes. that's more like it.
I'm untouched by the beauty of the evening.
Dusk descends too soon, obscuring my vision.
Ending my search,
While Morpheus casts
An early spell over my eyes.

POEM 16

Nature's Bounty

The sky is blushing, the birds are rushing,
Night's curtain will soon unravel,
The sun to another land will travel:
The purple cloud shrugs and sighs,
And hurriedly says a few good-byes,
As it won't be there when the sun returns,
So it cries and cries and cries . . .
Though it has no eyes . . .

POEM 17

The Passer by

Look at the cars pass by,
Each to its own destination,
Unknown to one another.
Gaze upon the clouds floating high
Up in the transient sky. Each moves with a mind
Impossible to find in the other.
How the leaves dance to the voice
Of the breeze, with impossible ease.
They sway, pause and croon, each
To its idiosyncratic tune
Sands of the desert waft, when
Currents of air with their well-worn craft
Scatter them. They disperse . . .
Each to its own destination,
unknown to one another.

POEM 18

The Wandering Mind

The heat was unbearable, the humidity terrible,
the curtains inadequate shields for the sun . . .
How was I to while away, this sultry, resinous April day?
Was there a way, if only one, to bear the burthen of this sun?

I picked up a book I never thought I would . . .
The front and back covers didn't seem too good.
'Not literary enough,' said my fine 'sensibility,'
this tome is trash, an unwanted liability . . .
But I felt brave, and flipped it open,
Romance I'd craved all morn you see . . .
And it did seem to me
that this book would be soppy enough to please me
Mushy enough to annoy and tease me
and apart from the irate comment or two, (or maybe 3)
it did mostly woo . . .
my mind. A most troubling yet gratifying find.
It did too help, that I
Imagined, *here I sigh*
an actor's form in the protagonist's role,
Down to the very last mole . . .
And I fished out romance from the most unsavoury parts,
and skilfully escaped the author's chosen darts . . .
He couldn't pin me down to his biases or opinions,
my imagination flew off on a pair of forged pinions . . .
What am I writing; oh for the sake of rhyming,
my mind is whining, I should be dining . . .

POEM 19

A Kiss in the Air

A kiss is flying through the air,
now it's entangled in my hair . . .
Why, it's staring me in the face,
It's moving again, what a pace,
But now it hovers, gently static,
Ecstatic . . .
Paralysed by its own fulfilment,
And yet,
Your eyes said nothing to me that night,
why did they seem
so hollow, so vacant, so bereft of sight?
I tried to penetrate their silent reticence,
but they remained unyielding, shielding
your thoughts. What nonsense
am I writing? When you
will do
nothing to
put my mind at ease?

POEM 20

Poetry in Nature

I stare blankly at the moon,
which holds no meaning for me now.
Not that it ever did,
coming to think of it.
I imagined, or rather hoped that
a poet in me would emerge, if I
could read strange things into it.
It could help embellish my poems,
like a pretty chain around one's neck.
A dangling ornament.
But it was too haughty, too evasive
and my metaphors too weak
and hackneyed.
Other poets have tampered with you enough.
And used you as a handy tool,
for supplying ready-made romance.
Maybe it's your soft-pearl glow
against night's impenetrable sky,
that touched many a sensitive soul,
whose quills, pens, key-boards,
reverberate with your name.
I'll turn to the stars instead,
and let you be for a while,
until I'm tempted
to use your alluring charm
one more time.
Just this once.

Winter Sunshine

Warmth within you which feeds my soul,
Engulfing the Cold Winds which did flow,
In harsh torrents, and lashing currents,
Before your light did glow . . . .
Slanting rays like the strings of a harp,
Enclose me in your music soft,
So I may croon your eternal tune,
When you are hidden by Star-time's loft . . .
O Spill some thoughts to guild my dreams,
With your beams of molten gold,
So I may muse, on Seas and shoes,
And on Sailors spinning yarns of old,
Which will remain forever untold . . .

POEM 22

Life is like that

What is life, unless it is filtered?
Through a many-hued prism?
What is a connection all about?
Unless it's been through a schism?
What does friendship really mean?
Unless it is tested by time?
What does harmony imply, if we
Cannot sift cacophony from a Chime?
As sweet as joy is the most bitter pill,
To a body which is weary and ill.
How a firm grasp of a gentle hand,
Energises and revives the will . . .
What does Love mean to you
On the loneliest of nights?
How is Companionship able
To reach unattainable heights?
How warm is the sense of security,
After being in the heart of a storm.
How nice it is to find ourselves,
After we've been out of form.
How soothing are the gathering clouds,
After a spell of Heat . . .
How welcome is the hardest chair,
After hours of being on our feet.

How do we measure the softness of a petal?
If not against the flower's thorn?
How do we mend something precious?
Unless it has been torn?
How purple is the evening haze,
When gazed upon with tired eyes.
How like music is a baby's laugh,
After enduring a night of cries.
How calming is a night of sleep,
After days and nights of unrest.
How important is kindness to a starved soul,
Its beauty surpasses all rest, being the best.
How thankful we are for a true, true friend,
When a frowning day is all but done.
Oh How rewarding it must be to unite,
With the chosen one.
What will happiness mean to us?
If we don't shed a bitter tear or two?
How drab will Life be indeed?
Unless it passes through unintended hues.

You'll Never Be Mine

Tonight I'll let you go,
Though you were never mine;
Tonight we're on our own, yet
I know that you'll be fine.
Tonight I heave a sigh,
As my green-dreams pass me by;
Silently disillusioned, I cry,
"Oh Dreams, you lie, you lie."
Tonight my eyes are wet,
But my mind is firm and set;
For, wait a while yet I won't
Since none of my needs were met.
(Just because I didn't have many,
Doesn't mean that I don't have any.)
Tonight I'm just, well, sad;
Though I have reasons to be glad;
There are so many more people to add,
On to the list of friends I've had.

Soon my eyes will be dry,
I'll no longer need to cry,
I'll no longer question "Why?"
As the days will pass me by.
They say Time heals all,
Even skin-marks left by a fall.
But Time alone will tell,
If it can mend a broken heart well.
Tonight I've set you free,
Will you never think of me?
Tonight I've let you go,
Though you were never mine.
Tonight we're on our own,
Will I really be fine?

POEM 24

The Bench

I sat upon a stone-worn bench,
When the day was all but done,
And Twilight dropped upon my shoulders,
As clouds embraced the retreating sun.
I felt terribly alone.
The world seemed so green and still, but
Broken whispers rode upon the breeze,
Unformed dreams danced hesitantly before my eyes.
The silence was pierced by earnest, quiet cries.
And all at once, I wasn't alone,
No, people were here before:
They'd dreamt, they'd sighed, they'd laughed, they'd cried,
They'd hoped, they'd feared, they'd quietly 'teared,'
They'd won, they'd lost, they'd loved, and they'd crossed,
Many rivers and seas, while they had lived.
And somehow,
Though I don't understand why,
(And I won't even try),
These strange thoughts cheered me on . . .

POEM 25

The Irrational Love

A mere glimpse, after many years
Washed away those silent fears,
Revealing,
That I still hold
The capacity for love,
Mostly Irrational,
Alwayyyys dysfunctional.
A hope too precious to articulate,
Tip-toes around the edges of my mind,
Until, inevitably, I find,
That your attention is elsewhere engaged.
But Hope doesn't seem to mind,
And alarmingly, unwittingly,
You Bind
Your soul to mine,
Oh unsuspecting Accomplice,
Contributing
To some inexplicable, inner bliss.

In Memory of Mrs Chatterjee

Your indelible memory
Will guide us from afar;
Softly shining always
Like a steady star.
. . . Whenever we'll feel the need,
To anchor our restless lives,
We'll search our souls for memories
Of you, where you're Blessing thrives.
Every once in a busy while,
We'll gaze upon the sky,
To remember you by the rainbow
Which chronicles the days gone by?
Often we'll feel disheartened and lost,
Often we'll feel pain . . .
But those lessons which we can never forget
Will restore and renew us again.
Though our paths will never cross,
We won't ever see your smile,
You'll be locked within our hearts,
To make our lives worth the while.

Wildflower

When Sleep will lead each of us
To the Deep end of the Dark,
You're far away words, your enlightening thoughts
Will blaze up from a spark.
I'm sorry that this poem is far from good,
It emerges from a vacuum within,
But you would have been nice about it nonetheless,
And encouraged me with your grin.
For I wrote poems all along,
Which were mostly far from good?
But the way you listened, so earnest and rapt,
I never quite understood,
How they were really so far from good.
And here I am, writing again,
By way of a humble tribute,
We bow before your brilliance, your kindness,
Which we'll forever salute.

POEM 27

The Startling Life

How startling is life, when we think of how . . .
It alters us, even now
I feel a change, somewhat strange,
Descend upon me like a settling cloud.
How Life flings us far away
From the very day
Of our birth . . . how it rents us apart
From our birth places . . .
Tears us away from those well-loved faces . . .
How it paints new chapters, with an invisible brush,
Sometimes ambling but forever in a rush . . .

POEM 28

For the Einstein at Einstein Centre

I was born with a forehead of wrinkles,
And a beard of the ripest gravy . . .
Each of my eyes wearily twinkles,
To welcome the visitors gay . . .
I am ageless, they say
I have been around for years,
My legs work tirelessly, bereft of choice.
I have also been deprived a voice.
My head is fixed at an awkward angle,
My jacket is a screaming green.
My characteristic shock of hair,
Dishevelled but clean.
I help people re-connect with their past,
Their days of childhood glory.
When they had seen me move up and down . . .
Some say, I'm lucky, with not a worry
In my mind . . . others say they're sorry
That I probably feel bored . . .

POEM 29

Love So Deep

I have tried so hard, so very hard
To love you to the brim,
To feel your joy and your pain,
Until my life grows dim
Having exhausted my feelings away.

POEM 30

The Sun the Moon and the Sea

In the haze of the noon,
I gaze upon
The traffic on the street,
The dust on tree leaves,
The smoke in the air,
But I find little to ensnare
Little reason to stop and stare.
I revert my thoughts to memories of a night,
A far away night in June,
Surrounded by the sound of the sea,
Under a luminous moon.
When the sky was a dense thicket of stars
And the clouds played hide and seek,
And the wind strummed a tune within my heart,
And nothing seemed dull and bleak.
When the sand yielded under my feet,
And engulfed me with its warmth,
And I lay in the company of unseen sea shells,
And awoke to the chime of distant Church bells.
Still of a mundane afternoon,
When I gaze upon the noon,
Though I may not see her in such splendour
I recall the luminous Sea-Moon.

POEM 31

A Riot of Disquiet

I am not happy, oh no I am not,
My mind is a riot of disquiet.
I am steeped in a sorrow so deep,
That I cannot reduce it to a weep.
I am not glad, oh no I am not,
With the agony of sadness all around,
How can I be happy in a world,
Where misery and anguish abound?
Every time a curtain is raised
And I chance a glimpse upon a soul,
I see their pain, I see them writhe,
Making it impossible to feel blithe.
The cacophony of Suffering pierces my ear,
As I watch the shedding of many a tear,
Some fall in silence, others ride on wails,
And my heart wildly flutters and quails.
Despair hurts many a sanguine heart,
Oh misery aims its skilful dart
At innocent and unsuspecting souls,
Cracking them into rugged shards.

POEM 32

Another Evening

The evening pulls me into myself,
In silent contemplation,
In exhaustive introspection,
In quiet, private, expectation,
I will wait for you.

Though the days are blurred and hurried,
Though the hours are capped with work,
Though my songs are left unwritten,
As they die upon my tongue,
Though my thoughts are still amorphous,
They crystallise at times,
When I convince myself,
That the wait is worth the while . . .

I have a life to carve,
I have a dream to shape,
It may take me a while,
To realise what it was,
I will spend my idle hours,
(Though there are very few,)
I will re-construct my desires,
And wait the while for you . . .

Debasree Ghosh

I have a while to work,
I have forever to learn,
We all have livings to earn,
But I shall not yearn
for you,
I shall instead,
Wait in well-rehearsed optimism . . .

So when walk past the lake of dreams,
Limpid with our love,
When we taste the bite of reality,
As we brush past its rude shove,
When we dance amidst the rainbow clouds of expectant
hopes,
When we avert our eyes from blazing, orange flames,
We'll be together, and our wait will be over at last.
If only for a while.

POEM 33

Reflection

Some nights are steeped in sequestered silence,
Some are submerged in infinite sadness . . .
while others are immeresed in epiphany
and euphoric gladness.
Some twilight hours are spent in thought,
While others are wasted and go to naught,
Some are sacred and are caught
In a spiritual web which cannot be bought,
Though it is constantly sought.
Some evening light is spent in peace,
When the clouds overhead are cotton and fleece,
And in the hour of a blessed sunset,
Sometime's one's eyelashes are wet,
With amorphous sorrow,
Which dissolves on the morrow.

POEM 34

The Journey Without an End

The circle of change inches forth,
Drawn by the ink of life,
Each experience a part of the compass,
Each hardship, happiness and strife.
Often we find that as we traverse,
We are back to where we begun,
Have we not then forged ahead,
Has the race then not been run?
Thoughts like these might mislead
Us, into thinking the journey is futile,
For what are the measurable results
If we haven't covered the extra mile?
But all at once a message dawns
In the crevices of the mind,
A thought that washes doubts away,
Being one of its kind.
For it's hardly about the journey without,
Rather the one within,
How far have we probed deep inside,
And let ourselves profoundly in?
How many acres of soul
Have we explored and scrutinized?
How many aspects of ourselves
Have we realized?

Have we understood our Reason for Being,
The purpose we are here to fulfill?
For that calling resides in our hearts
The world is but the window-sill.
How much have we learned along the way,
What epiphany has charmed our nights?
How precious has the learning curve been,
As we scale Empyrean heights?
Or dip into valleys low?
Whether our pace is fast or slow?
Active or reflective?
Bustling or contemplative?
What do we take along with us,
If at all we do?
What has become so ingrained in our selves,
That losing it, we will rue?
What do we leave behind,
But a little bit of ourselves,
The bit we have let out to the world,
That is not hiding behind opaque shelves
Of society and image,
Which shield and bandage,
Our inner beings from the glare of the world.

The Stream

Old Mar. Hanshaw had his face turned towards the wall, as he lay on his bed, living on borrowed time. 70 years had passed by, almost in a jiffy, he thought. But it must have taken AGES, he reasoned with himself, to have built up the repository of memories which were now reposing in quiet corners of his furiously active brain. He no longer felt keenly about the absence of books by his bed-side. It was enough for him to turn over the chapters which were strewn across his mind, and attempt to string them together, in some semblance of chronology.

The doctor had merely given a grave, subtle little nod to the Nurse, that morning. She thought Old Mar. Hanshaw, as he was popularly known, was too ill to realize the dark significance of her little gesture. But Mar. Hans haw's eyes had always been sharp, and he felt a sharp pain slice his insides, with the sharp jaggedness of a serrated-edged knife.

The world was far too precious to him. He had NEVER taken it for granted. He'd be up at five, to keenly welcome each morning, he'd sing a silent ode to the hottest of afternoons, sitting at his office cubicle, he'd worship each evening's ephemeral loveliness, and he would anticipate each new night with the exhilarated eagerness of a love-cloaked girl, awaiting a letter from her beloved.

His thoughts were always with HER. She was by his side, every waking moment, and every sleeping hour. She nestled against him in the soft hours of those lonesome nights; she was holding his hands, with her feathery fingers, in the first hours of the Dawn, when the Dark Curtains of the previous Night were parting, to make way for a brand new day, a brand new scene. She was with him, as he stirred his porridge in his lonely kitchen, as he bent over slightly to see if he had boiled it enough. Her fingers fluttered nimbly, over his, as he turned the pages of the morning Newspaper. She hovered around, like a formless Angel, when he dressed hurriedly, to get ready for work. When he arrived breathless at the bus stop, she would inspire him with her indefatigably energetic spirit. On afternoons, when his clerical duties seemed never-ending, she would infuse him with an enthusiasm so rare, that the people around him wondered at his passion for the monotonous tasks he so smilingly performed.

The evenings were the most Special of All. She would stroke his hair, mop his brow, and effortlessly glide into his soul, as effortlessly as the gentle, sudden transition, with which the sky went from blue-pink-pitch black and star-studded, with a quiet certainty. No, he was never alone. Yes, she was always there, the Moonshine Girl, the Healer of the Spirit, the Stimulator of all things lovely, the girl he had never had the courage to speak to. And yet, he was never alone. Maybe that's why he was never alone. Yet, she was never a figure of Exasperating Idealism, which a lot of women become to single men. She was real, she had faults . . . oh yes, she and Hans haw would argue in his mind, over a plethora of trivial issues . . . and the end of each session, Hans haw would leave a silent rose on his window-sill, to make up for his recalcitrance . . . the first sign of madness, some had said. Mad, had Hans haw smirked. Who could be labelled as completely sane?

His thoughts drifted even further back, to his mother. The flowers on the table she so carefully arranged, the loose bun on her head, which she so carelessly tied. The warm smell of her gentle, sudden hugs, the lopsided half smile which danced upon her lips when he returned home with his sports trophies. Her love of all food bland, her love for sad, sad movies, which made her silently cry into her pink, pink handkerchief, while the little Mar. Hans haw watched on, in great distress (he did not like to see his mother cry, but she so often did, thinking he wouldn't notice), such thoughts came hurtling back to him now, with the speed of an over-zealous train.

His Father. What memories did he have? Mar. Hans haw tried to turn out his mind, as he would turn out his pockets on his birthdays, when he would receive sweets from his friends. Yes, his father. He had been a big, busy man, busy doing things which Hans haw had no idea about. He was hardly ever in the house. He hardly spoke to mother. He was hardly ever there. But Hans haw did remember the rough sting of his father's one brusque kiss on his cheek, the only form of affection he ever showed, before he left with that brown, or was it grey suit-case. Did the colour matter now? Had it ever mattered? How old had he been, Hans haw? Seven? Eight? Nine? Did it matter anymore? But that was the end of the Father-chapter. Did he miss his father? Did he judge him harshly in his later years? Hanshaw never did. A father was a father to him, if irresponsible, if callous, if cruel, a father was a father. Hanshaw frowned in the Darkness. These were not his words. These had been his Mother's last words.

Not of mother, though, no. Mother was always there, sadder still after father left, but somehow happier too.

But what about the University degree? Mar. Hanshaw could never complete it. Blame it all on the broken leg, he thought. But a clerk's job was not a bad one, someone had to do the work, he'd reasonable reasoned with himself.

His office cubicle had been quite a sight to behold. Cluttered one day, organized the next, cluttered one day, and re-organized the next. And the books of poetry . . . what poetry did to Hanshaw, a bowl of hot soup did to a sore throat, a cool strip of cloth did to a warm, fevered fore-head, a good night's sleep did to a worn-out body and mind.

Which quote was playing upon his mind now? No, it was not the one he thought would play in his last hours. "Do not go gentle into that good night . . ." For Hanshaw had ALWAYS been a gentle man, ready to succumb, ready to yield, and ALWAYS ready to re-adjust. No, he had been delusional in thinking Dylan would win over Keats . . .

"Now, more than ever it seems rich to die . . ."

And slowly, the jagged knife inside him melted, as though the pain of his imminent extinction was being extinguished by an unseen, cool, soothing balm . . .

And then there was John Clare, whose "I AM" was embedded in his mind forever . . . a sudden flash . . . three boys who had taunted him by calling him fat . . . Hanshaw shedding tears . . . the boys laughing . . . and She, silently reprimanding the boys, smiling shyly at Hanshaw and running away . . . that had been her last day at school . . .

Mad, they had called him, mad Old Hanshaw, MAD in his recent days. Why, he thought? Because he spoke to the birds which perched upon the balcony of the Home? Why, because he remained silent for long, long spells, lost in his realm of memories and dreams? Why, because he refused to eat for three days, as he wanted the poor, thin-as-a-rail lady on the next bed, to have his helping as well. So what if she was not allowed to eat solid food, as they had explained to him. Did they ever really matter, the states of matter? What was the state of his life now? Was he about to assume the gaseous state of diffuse nothingness when his solid body would be laid to rest, soil heaped over it? Were the years in between Liquid, flowing from one incident to the next, and one state of existence to another?

He remembered his Physics tutor. He had such huge spectacles. And he detested poetry. What was his name? Hanshaw didn't pursue this thought. It hadn't mattered then. It certainly didn't matter now.

All his life, Mr. Hanshaw had wanted to write a book. It was his only regret. His only regret. But now, in his last waking hours, he realized that all books were not written by hand, there were a few which were authored by Life.

Just A Happy Love Story . . .

Paranthetical Insertion

Sheena cast a surreptitious glance at the boy seated next to her. She was inwardly fuming and flaming at the thought of being forced into this hasty alliance. Aunty Rita sat opposite them, her face caked with make-up, her heavily shadowed azure eyelids glimmering in the sunlight which streamed into the room. "We told you she was very striking," she was saying while nodding her head vigorously in Sheena's direction. Ma and Baba stood quietly in one corner, a little bewildered by the alacrity with which things were moving. Sheena took one glance at them and felt irritated. What was the point of feeling surprised now? Why hadn't her father worked harder to deflect this 'appointment,' as she had expected him too? And WHAT was the deal with her mother's exasperatingly vacillating expressions?

Uncles Anu and Ajay had taken their usual posts at the table, and were eagerly supervising the laying of the table by the aged and rather crusty workers at their house. "You must try Babu's biriyani," Uncle Anu hollered across the living room., while Ajay urged Babu to serve the guests with his signature mint and rose syrup. The boy's mother looked directly, too directly at Sheena, or so it seemed to Sheena's parents, whose anxious expressions belied their forced smiles and nods.

Sheena wiped her forehead. She'd taken great care to look as unkempt and care-worn as possible. Her hair was tied up in the most casual of buns, something she knew her parents hated. She'd deliberately left her eyes un-smeared with kajol, and she was wearing an old t-shirt and skirt which she had long since relegated to antiquity. What Sheena didn't realize was that her casual elegance was serving the perverse purpose of heightening her attractiveness. Her sandal-tinted cheeks looked flushed with anger and embarrassment, her eyes shone a little too brightly in silent rebellion and her tense body gave her a charm that was at once appealing, alluring and somehow dangerous.

The boy looked almost as uncomfortable as Sheena felt. His dark hair was frequently smoothened by a rather nervous hand, and he kept his eyes trained on the floor. He seemed to be surveying the carpet with great attention. Aunty Rita took this as an opportunity for sparking off a novel conversation. "This is from Iran. Sheena went there last year to visit her Married friend Natasha!" said Aunty Rita, wiggling her finger emphatically and adding unnecessary stress on what she felt was a significant word. Sheena sighed. That trip, with its myriad memories had ceased to conjure pleasant images in her mind, ever since she'd heard of Natasha's unceremonious separation from her husband. It had been no one person's fault. After the first rosy veneer of illusions had faded away, they had been left with nothing to carry on with. Sheena hadn't understood at first. Weren't people supposed to make an effort? How come Natasha and her husband didn't realize this acrid truth during those two years of incessant phone calls and finger-numbing text-messages? How come they used to go out on those dates to expensive restaurants and movie halls? How could they have expected to get to know one another if they never really communicated with one another? They were always surrounded by people wherever they went, and it was as though they were serving some larger purpose by dating, contributing to the popular, prevailing culture somehow. But Sheena did not want to be too judgmental. It was always easier to analyze from an objective distance. Real life situations always have the ability to throw people horribly off-guard. And Sheena began to feel that she was thinking too much about the whole affair while Natasha was moving on quicker. Sheena's sensitive and over-empathizing nature was making her more bitter than either Natasha or her husband.

The boy's mother pricked up her ears at the mention of Iran. "Iran . . . Tehran is such a lovely city. Do you remember Akash how your daddy and I took you there when you were 9?" exclaimed the lady with a dreamy expression in her eyes. Sheena looked into them for the first time since they'd entered their house. They were so warm, so soft and so, so liquid, Sheena felt herself thinking. Her eyes seemed to be pensively picturing the mist-clad mountains of far-away Tehran, where she'd been secure and happy in the company of her husband and child. Sheena felt suddenly moved, somehow suddenly touched. She glanced again at the boy next to her and saw him looking shyly at her. He would have hurriedly turned his face away had she not smiled.

It was only yesterday that Aunty Rita had bounced into their house with this laugh of a proposal. She had a notorious reputation for being a passionate binder of hearts, but so far Sheena had managed to escape unscathed. She was always so serious and studious, so impossibly and remotely romantic, that neither she nor her family members ever bothered about pairing her up in reality. Sheeena was content to satisfy her own romantic yearnings through works of literature and films. She was growing up, but not quite, not being one to renounce her hold on childhood that easily. What difference did a few measly years make when THERe was still plenty of time to behave like a full-on grown up she figured.

Well, so Sheena didn't keenly feel the lack of a boyfriend, though she did have her wistful moments. It was never really peer pressure that got to her. It was more the phenomenon of sudden bursts of anxiety over whether she would eventually meet her soul-mate and be able to recognize him to be the "one." She wasn't crazy enough to expect him to appear on a steed of gold, with accompanying fanfare and music . . . rather she hoped for someone who'd love her forever in a quiet, steady and rather loyal way. Oh yes, and it would help if she found him a teeny bit good looking.

So there was Aunty Rita, her rapidly ageing face dolled up as usual, puffing and panting into the house. Sheena had just finished typing out her latest application essay when her mother's happy laugh greeted her ears. "And why not? Whenever he wishes!" Sheens heard her exclaim. "What are you talking about?" Sheena demanded as she climbed down the stairs to the living room where her mother was serving Aunty Rita with tea and her favorite Marie biscuits. "There is someone Rita-di would like you to meet . . . someone special," her mother giggled like a hopeless teenager. Something inside Sheena squirmed and she glared at her mother in anger. "I thought I told you N-EVER to fix up or arrange anything for me mommy," she exclaimed, aiming her comment towards Aunty Rita. Aunty Rita was not one to be deterred so easily. "It's not like you have a boyfriend or anything . . . let this just be a trial . . . who knows? You might even end up dating him." She retorted. "Oh, I'm the first victim of your latest project, the blind dating academy?" Sheens found herself exclaiming, much to her horror. She'd always been so polite, especially around relatives, but she could not help feeling distraught and distressed. Aunty Rita was suddenly making her feel so hopelessly inadequate, as though she felt Sheena was incapable of garnering a boyfriend for herself. In fact, it was the ever-prudent Sheena who always turned down proposals from boys she found unsuitable. Anyway. Sheena rather dramatically turned on her heels and stormed out of the room. Her mother, who had been trying in vain to establish a modicum of peace between the two, wrung her hands in despair and rather dramatically collapsed on the nearest sofa.

Sheena had run up to her room and flipped open her newly acquired pink laptop. She'd not allow any kind of artificial arrangement, which was altogether too business-like for Sheena's taste, deter her lofty ideals of romance. She made up her mind to be as difficult and stubborn as possible. Aunt Rita seemed exceedingly shallow and intrusive to her at the moment . . . and her temporary wave of anger made her forget for a while just how well-meaning and honest-intentioned a woman Aunt Rita was. She was a rather lonely lady, who had lost her children in a long-ago car crash. Her husband had decided to abandon her when she'd given birth to a second daughter. Aunty could have become a bitter cynic. But she'd decided to carry on with life . . . her unhappy past had curiously re-in forced her faith in God, and she had committed herself to helping others the best she could. "I literally want to bring colour into lives!" she'd exclaimed, when a few baffled people had criticized and questioned her decision to "always put on so much make up, that too given her tragic circumstances . . ." Some people dismissed her as insane, others found her eccentric, some found her heartless and uncaring . . . both those few lives which she was able to touch were never the same.

The next day was cloudy and rather grey. Sheena was rather annoyed. She loved savoring days when the weather was tempestuous, but today was already marred by Aunty Rita and her strangely concurring parents. However, she had to admit, if only to herself, that she was feeling slightly nervous and somehow excited. A part of her was curious, the part which made the butterflies flutter in her stomach. But she didn't exactly know what to attribute this feeling to, and so rather tiredly began the seemingly arduous task of getting dressed.

Akash was feeling out of sorts that morning. His forehead felt unnaturally warm and his eyes seemed to sting. "Drat!" he said to himself as he looked out of the window near his head. A rainy and depressing day, he thought, just the kind he disliked. It was time for him to get dressed and head to someone's place. Someone who might turn out to be a life-partner, a soul-mate. Akash usually kept an open mind about most things. Ever since he had returned from the U.S. he realized it probably was time to settle down to the idea of 'settling down.' He had always had a very strong paternal instinct latent within him. He loved playing with small children at family gatherings and parties, where they would inevitably flock to him like bees to honeyed flowers. Maybe his soft, velvety brown eyes were particularly enchanting to little kids who insisted on crawling all over his lap, requested him for stories and took turns to ride on his shoulders. Of late his thoughts seemed to be centered excessively around children. Maybe his father's death had had something to do with it. He remembered how wonderful and caring a parent his father had been and perhaps wished to re-connect with his lost father by becoming one himself. Often he found himself wishing he'd become a pediatrition instead of a cardiac surgeon.

He thought of the vacant years which lay ahead of them . . . his father had been inseparable from his mother. So much so that sometimes even Akash felt himself feel like an intruder, in their company. His parents were never aware of it themselves, but every unconscious gesture or look on their parts suggested that they had lost themselves in one another. Akash often came home to a dreary house now, with his mother burying her face among the heaps of his father's shirts in a cupboard. She had refused to emerge from her room for days, until Aunty Rita, her mother's new neighbor, had really drawn her out. It was a surprising camaraderie, but it worked wonders for Mrs. Ghosh. Aunt Rita actually taught her to look back on her husband's memories in fond remembrance, and to celebrate their years of togetherness, rather than solely lament for him. The very mention of his name no longer made her want to torture herself with agonized tears, but brought a sudden gush of instant happiness and a bitter-sweet smile to her face. More importantly, and perhaps strangely, she never felt his absence any longer. Somehow he was always with her, and she knew exactly what he was saying, and how he was helping her. She even surprised herself by regaining bits of her old, rather wicked, rather perplexing sense of humor. Akash was much relieved, and often marveled at Aunt Rita's capacity to work wonders. She seemed to have spilled some carefully preserved sunshine into their suddenly darkened lives, without even having known his father. Had never even seen him. Some inexplicable things can really make a difference, Mrs. Ghosh thought.

Akash shook his head. His long working hours had begun to take their toll on him, and he found himself without an appetite at the breakfast table. His mother looked concerned and a bit jittery herself. "What's up, Akash? Not feeling well?" she said as Akash fidgeted with his porridge. "No I'm fine, just a little un-hungry," he grinned, not wishing to worry his mom. "I think you need a break . . . you're wearing yourself out with your work. I've been telling you so for ages." Akash sighed. "Mom, you know doctors can't afford to be lazy or lax . . . you know how I feel about this, ever since dad . . ." his voice trailed off slowly and his tired eyes met his mother's moist ones. "Sorry ma," Akash reached over and patted his mother's arm "see, I've taken this day off and have agreed to accompany you, without even a hint of an argument." "You're looking much too pale for a prospective groom and your hand feels clammy . . . maybe we should just call it off for the day? Let's go catch a movie or something?" his mom anxiously suggested. "Come on mom, I'm not that sick . . . you know I hate going to claustrophobic movie halls!" Akash grinned wanly as he left the table to get ready.

They had hailed a cab to the Bannerjee's residence. Mrs. Ghosh would not hear of her son driving that day. She was not entirely certain if she was doing the correct thing by trying to arrange a marriage for her son. She had immense faith in love marriages owing to her own idyllic years with Ratan, her husband and companion of many years. Even as a young girl she'd never had much faith in the arranged marriage concept. If it worked, fine . . . even love marriages involved risks and chances . . . but the whole idea of putting two strangers, who knew not the first thing about one another, under the pressure of a marriage seemed bizarre. But she knew Akash was lonely, was too shy to garner a girlfriend for himself, and she also knew that he secretly craved his mother to find someone for him. She probably felt more nervous that her son, who was leaning back in his seat and trying to catch a quick nap.

Sheena didn't know what to think. The guy's mother was really nice, she thought. After a few moments of customary awkwardness, they'd struck up an interesting conversation. She discovered Mrs. Ghosh's love for Leonard Cohen and L.M. Montgomery. "I grew up on a healthy diet of Lucy Maud's books . . . and I even got my husband and son hooked to them," she smiled in fond remembrance . . . "much as he might not admit it now," she continued, glancing at Akash, who had turned a bright shade of crimson. Sheena looked at him and he felt he that should try to release his tongue from the fetters of silence, and say something to her. "So are you studying Literature? That's what Aunty Rita told mom yesterday! It's such a fascinating field." He managed to say. Sheena smiled, without looking at him. His eyes were too intense and she suddenly faltered under his gaze. "Umm . . . yes, it is . . ." she managed to mumble. "Why don't you take him up to your room and talk in peace?" Aunty Rita chimed in, wishing to push things as much as she could manage. She was delighted that things seemed to be taking off. Sheena glanced at her parents. Her mother gave her a little encouraging smile and the slightest nod, while her father looked away, embarrassed. He just couldn't come to terms with the fact that his little child was old enough to be considered 'marriagiable.'

Sheena led the way upstairs. Akash followed rather hesitantly, as his head had begun to throb again. He was now beginning to feel more than a little alarmed with the whole episode, and was suddenly feeling confused and dazed. What if this attractive girl had a boyfriend? What if he was about to listen to an unceremonious rejection in her room? What if she found him a dismal and dull person, not worthy to be spoken to? Sure, he'd had lots of friends of both sexes, but he suddenly felt as though he'd never had a single conversation in his life before . . . he felt devoid of speech, blank and vague. He forgot that he was a lovely, fun person to be around, that he was a brilliant conversationalist, with a unique sense of humor. So he walked into Sheena's look feeling every bit the nervous wreck, without realizing that Sheena was feeling much the same.

Akash leaned against the wall and looked out of the window. The rain was really pouring down now, making visibility difficult. "I love the luscious rains!" Sheena said dreamily, feeling a bit more relaxed. "You're looking as perplexed as I feel!" she exclaimed with a laugh. Sheena had a sudden, infectious and rather delicious laugh. Akash looked at her and smiled, feeling his apprehension melt away, by 'soft degrees.' "Why don't you sit down?" Sheena said and pulled up a soft, cushiony chair. "After you," Akash said softly. Sheena sat down by the edge of her bed and Akash lowered himself on to the chosen seat.

"I don't know how you feel about this whole thing . . ." Sheena found herself saying. This boy was alarmingly good looking, in a very unusual sort of way, she thought. She found herself being enveloped in a cloud of diffidence and began to stammer a little. "I . . . It is not as if I'm . . . I mean I've never been . . . it might sound strange . . . but I've . . . you know . . . never really been in this situation, or in a relationship before this . . . not that I'm labeling ours as . . . I mean . . . I don't know what I mean . . ." Sheena finished with a gasp. What was she saying? He must think her awfully stupid and not in the least like the powerful speaker an English major ought to be. Akash's eyes laughed but he kept a straight face . . . "Are you an expert in legilemency apart from literature? I mean, you just echoed my thoughts verbatim!" he smiled, and found himself feeling rather paralyzed by Sheena's casual charm and her unpretentious personality and her intelligent yet innocent way of speaking. Her eyes were so hypnotic that Akash had to force himself to look away for a bit. Sheena somehow knew she could trust this lad. She didn't know why, but she just knew it, with a confidence she'd never felt before. He came across as one of those instinctively pleasant people. What they both begun to secretly realize that they were both young, romantic and hungry for love, and they might just end up being wrapped up in that emotion. They might have things in common, they might discover a multitude of differences, they might have quarrels, they might hurt one another, but they both suddenly hoped they'd stick with one another, no matter what . . . idealistic yet practical . . . or so they thought to themselves . . .

"I haven't been too well today," Akash disclosed. "Oh I'm sorry to hear that!," Sheena exclaimed genuinely concerned. "Would you like to lie down for a bit?" she said. "It won't be awkward!" she quickly added. "No it's fine . . . I'm just feeling a little bit over-strained!" he confessed. "I have always loved the medical profession. But you mustn't work yourself too hard . . ." she added gently. "It's what I use to keep myself distracted . . . ever since my own father . . . passed on . . . and I was called back from the U.S. it's been a tad difficult . . ." Akash never confided in people easily, but somehow Sheena already felt like a kindred spirit. The fact that they were expected to become husband and wife didn't exert any pressure on him . . . in fact, that knowledge coupled with his instinctive feelings towards Sheena somehow made it easier for him. Sheena had always been a good listener, and she'd often dreamt of the day when she might assume the role of her beloved's confidante, whom she would be able to help and care for . . . whose feelings she'd respect and be respected in return. Sheena's heart warmed to Akash who spoke in such an earnest way, so as to not demand sympathy or attention. He gave her a candid account of his hopes and desires, to help people who were unwell, to see his mother happy, to perhaps be a good parent someday. Sheena blushed. She loved children too . . . she thought nothing as sacred as motherhood . . . and she gently broke these feelings to an elated Akash. "I've always earnestly believed that motherhood should never be an imposition on women," she explained rather confusedly. "I mean, it should always be allowed to remain a choice. A woman who does not want to be a mother should not be labeled an aberration by those who do . . . . I've always wanted children for myself . . . but I see why some women might not!" she finished. Akash nodded rather seriously . . . "I know what you mean . . . only I could never phrase it as eloquently as you just did."

Sheena secretly thanked God that she had refrained from following the paths of some of her, well rather unrestrained friends, who changed boyfriends every week, till the novelty of romance completely wore out for them. If she had succumbed to peer-pressure, would she have felt as 'blythe'-spirited as she was feeling now? Akash, too, had always been teased for being too idealistic and romantic, by his friends. "Just cease the day and grab a chick," one rather offensive guy had once told him . . . "But doesn't she have to be the right one?" Akash had rather emphatically asked. "Is ANYONE ever the right one?" the guy had said, throwing him an exasperated look. "Well, at least I have to be deluded into thinking she is!" Akash had responded before turning away. Now it seemed as though he had deluded himself enough to work up an appetite for the pilaf that awaited them downstairs.